ROBBIE THE ROOSTER
A TALE OF
SAM & JACK'S
FISHING FOLLY

Carmen Elizabeth lives in the mountains of Spain with her husband, two cats and three goldfish. She enjoys writing stories for her grandchildren. This is the first of five books.

Carmen Elizabeth

Published
by
Bonkerbooks

A catalogue record for this book is available from the British
Library

ISBN 978-0-9929144-3-1
www.Bonkerbooks.com
For the preservation of World Wildlife

Carmen Elizabeth

One lovely weekend, Sam had his best friend, Jack staying over at his grandparent's farm. Now Jack was as mischievous as Sam, but they had both promised to be good and on their best behaviour. Listening through the open window, Robbie thought be good, best behaviour, oh yes! Maybe one day!

After breakfast Sam and Jack were chatting about what they would like to do after helping grandad feed the hens.

"I know," Jack said, "how about going fishing in the stream?" The stream at bottom of the field was a short way from the farmhouse.

"What a great idea of yours," Sam called back to Jack. "Grandad, do you know if our buckets and nets still hanging in the barn?"

"Yes," grandad called back, "we have to go through the barn to feed Robbie and the hens. We can pick them up then."

Gran made up a snack of crisps, with some delicious cake which she had made the day before, also a drink for them. Gran told them not to go any further than the stream. "Remember, the river is just a short way from the stream so be sensible, stay where I can see you both from the window."

"Ok gran," they both called back.

Going through the barn, where Robbie and the hens were waiting patiently for their breakfast, Jack and Sam spread the corn on the floor outside. Grandad unhooked the nets and buckets from the barn shelf.

Looking up from his corn Robbie, wondered what kind of mischief they both was getting into now. The last time they both went fishing, they had a mud fight and came back covered in mud.

What an awful sight that was, gran wasn't too pleased with them that day. Robbie decided that after his breakfast he would follow them down to the stream.

When Sam and Jack got to the stream they sat on the grass and started to eat their snacks. Even though they had not long had their breakfast, they decided it was better to carry their snacks in their tummies rather than in their bags. After they both had finished eating, they put their nets into the stream.

"Let's see who can catch the most fish;" Sam said, "there are lots of little fish swimming around."

After a while they both had quite a lot of fish in their bucket. Robbie looked inside the bucket, fascinated as the fish swam around and around, he got quite dizzy watching them.

After a while Sam got bored with such small fish. "I know," he said to Jack, "let's go to the river it's only a short walk down from the stream."

" I don't know," said Jack, "we told gran we would be good."

"We will." called Sam, while running alongside the stream towards the river.

Oh no, thought Robbie, as he strutted along behind them, this sounds like a big trouble to me!

When Sam and Jack reached the river they saw it was higher than usual. Forgetting it had rained the day before making the bank very slippery, but this did not stop them from trying to catch a couple of big fish they saw swimming by the side of the river bank.

"We could catch one for dinner," called Sam.

"Yeah," Jack agreed, "gran could cook us some chips to go with it." They both loved chips.

Tipping out their bucket, letting the fish slide down the bank into the river, Robbie thought they looked just like large worms, but too fast to catch, as they slithered away and out of reach.

Jack and Sam made so much noise that they scared all the fish away. This did not stop Sam from putting his net into the water. Just then, Sam slipped but managed to catch hold of a broken tree branch.

"Jack help me out, my welly's are stuck!"

Sam suddenly realised if he moved any more there was a good chance he would fall into the water. Though he had his 25 metre swimming certificate he would not like to try swimming in the river.

"Go and get grandad Jack!"

Robbie squawked and squawked. Jack started to panic and crying, ran as fast as his legs would carry him towards the farm.

Grandad knew something was wrong when he saw Jack running towards the tractor without Sam.

Grandad turned the tractor off and Jack began to tell him what had happened.

"Jump on Jack." Turning the engine back on, Jack had his finger crossed all would be well, now he had grandad with him. When they got to the river, Robbie was still squawking. Robbie knew they were both naughty and in big trouble but would not like to see them get hurt.

Grandad was able to hold onto the branch and managed to pull Sam up onto the bank. Sam was shaking, by this time both wellington's had fallen off and went whizzing down the river and sunk.

"That could have been you Sam," Grandad was very cross with them both for not being sensible and not doing as gran had told them.

Robbie was still squawking, when grandad shouted out "Robbie if you don't stop squawking, I'll get gran to make a pie out of you."

Robbie ran off in disgust, a pie out of me, whatever next! So he went to tell all the other animals the trouble Sam and Jack had got into, although they had been very silly Robbie was very pleased that both boys were alright.

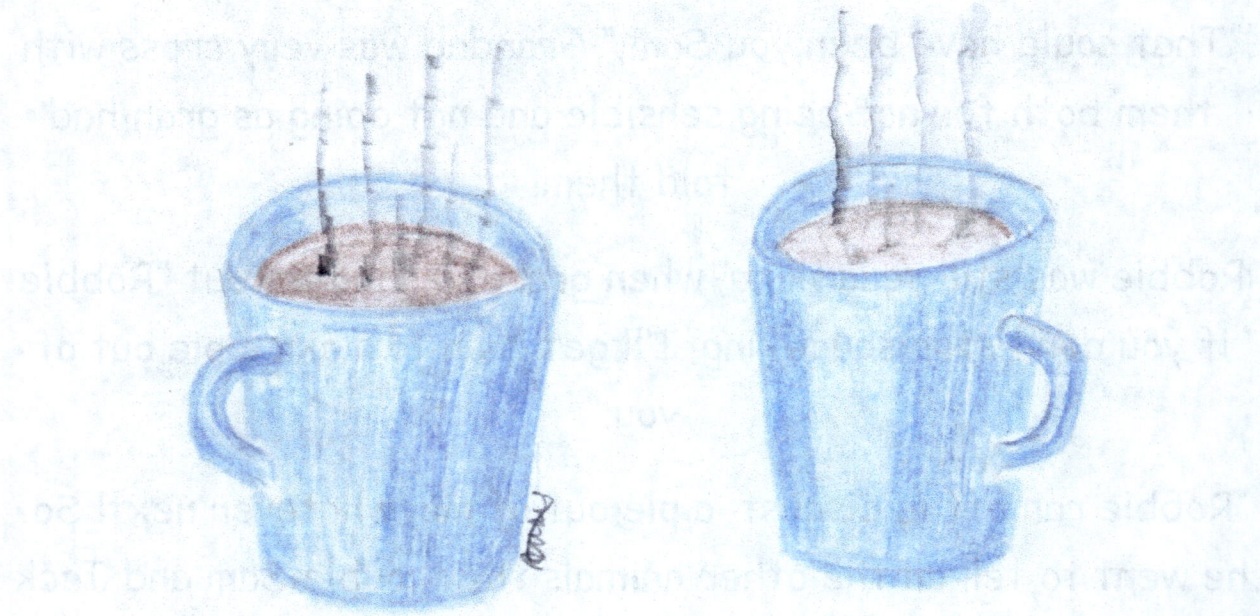

When grandad returned to the farm, gran was waiting for them in the kitchen with a hot drink.

"You are both very silly, I trusted you to be good, and you could have both drowned and disappeared like your wellington boots that sunk.

Even the most strongest of swimmers may have found themselves in trouble today. What will your mums and dads think of you? They will not be very pleased with your behaviour. I hope you have learnt a valuable lesson today?"

More of Robbie's adventures to come